Tippy-Toe
Chick, GO!

By George Shannon

Tippy-Toe Chick, GO!

Pictures by Laura Dronzek

Greenwillow Books, An Imprint of HarperCollinsPublishers

Acrylic paints were used for the full-color art.
The text type is Korinna.

Library of Congress Cataloging-in-Publication Data

Shannon, George.
Tippy-toe chick, go! / by George Shannon ;
illustrated by Laura Dronzek.
p.   cm.
"Greenwillow Books."
Summary: When a mean dog blocks the path to the garden
where a delicious breakfast awaits, Little Chick shows her family
how brave and clever she is.
ISBN 0-06-029823-5 (trade). ISBN 0-06-029824-3 (lib. bdg.)
[1. Chickens—Fiction. 2. Dogs—Fiction. 3. Courage—Fiction.]
I. Dronzek, Laura, ill. II. Title.
PZ7.S5288 Ti 2003   [E]—dc21   2002017509

10 9 8 7 6 5 4 3 2   First Edition

For Doris, Kaitlyn,
& Mary Stuart Shannon
—G. S.

For Susan, Virginia,
Ava, & Phyllis
—L. D.

Every morning when the dew had dried,
Hen took her chicks to the garden for their favorite
treat—sweet itty-bitty beans and potato bugs.

Hen, Big Chick, and Middle Chick next,

with Little Chick trailing along behind.

Stopping to wonder   at this   and that.

Then running,   *tippy-toe, tippy-toe,*   to catch the rest.

Across the yard. Into the garden to eat, eat, eat.

Every day, every day of the week.

Till **ONE** day—

RUFF-RUFF-<small>RUFF</small>-<small>RUFF</small>-RUFF!

A big, grumpy dog came running their way, barking and growling at the end of a rope.

Hen jumped back and pulled her chicks near. "There's no safe way to the beans today. We'll just have to wait for chicken feed."

All three chicks said, "Bleck!" and frowned.

"We're hungry!"

"You PROMISED!"

"We DID our chores!"

Hen sighed. "But we'll NEVER get past a dog like that."

Big Chick said, "Wait. I'LL take care of this."

He slowly took a step toward Dog.

"Now listen," he called. "We won't hurt you.

We're just going to the garden for an itty-bitty treat."

RUFF-RUFF-RUFF-**RUFF-**RUFF!
Dog disagreed, barking and pulling
at the end of his rope.
Big Chick ran to hide under Hen's safe wing.

Middle Chick took a breath, then stepped toward Dog.
"I'M hungry, so YOU'D better stop it right now!
Or YOU'LL be sorry when we get hold of you."

RUFF-RUFF-ruff-RUFF-RUFF!

Dog disagreed, barking and pulling at the end of his rope.

Middle Chick ran to hide under Hen's safe wing.

"Let's go," said Hen. "We'll really have to wait."
Little Chick peeped, "*I* want to try."

"Oh, no!" said Hen, as the other chicks laughed.
"You're much too small."

Little Chick yelled, "But *I* can RUN!"
And off she went, *tippy-toe, tippy-toe,*
as fast as she could. Straight toward Dog.

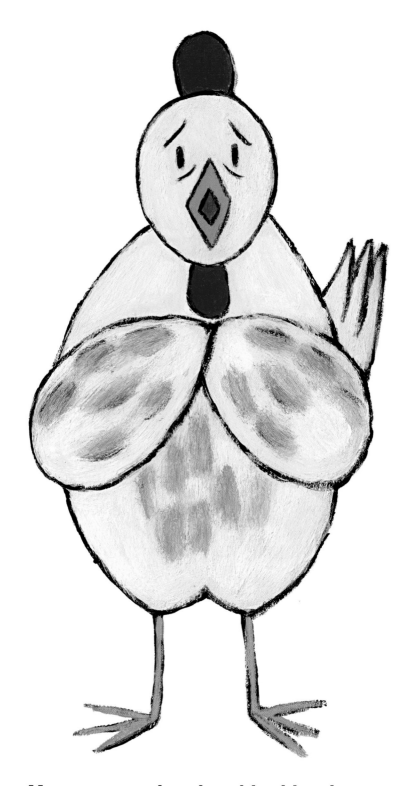

Hen screamed and grabbed her heart.

Big Chick closed his eyes.

Middle Chick shook.

Little Chick ran,
tippy-toe, tippy-toe,
without stopping to rest
till she felt Dog's breath.

Then Little Chick laughed
and began to run again.
Tippy-toe, tippy-toe
around the tree.

Dog chased after her,
tugging at his rope.
RUFF-RUFF-RUFF-
RUFF-RUFF!

Tippy-toe, tippy-toe
around the tree.
Tippy-toe, tippy-toe, tippy . . .
RUFF-RUFF-**RUFF!**

Around and around,
tippy-toe,
tippy-toe.
Till . . .

RUFF-RUP**-yip-**
yip-yip-yip!
Dog's rope was wrapped
all around the tree.
He was stuck, and too mad
to think "back up."

Hen clucked with pride.

Big Chick and Middle Chick just stood and stared.

Little Chick called,

"It's time to eat!"

And off they ran, *tippy-toe, tippy-toe*. Right past Dog and into the

garden for their favorite treat—sweet itty-bitty beans and potato bugs.

YUM!